To Holly

With our love,

Barbara & Arthur Currie xx

THE
BEST EVER
NURSERY RHYMES
& TALES

THE
BEST EVER
NURSERY RHYMES
& TALES

Illustrated and Tales Retold by

Jonathan Langley

HarperCollins *Children's Books*

Contents

THE
BEST EVER
NURSERY RHYMES

CONTENTS

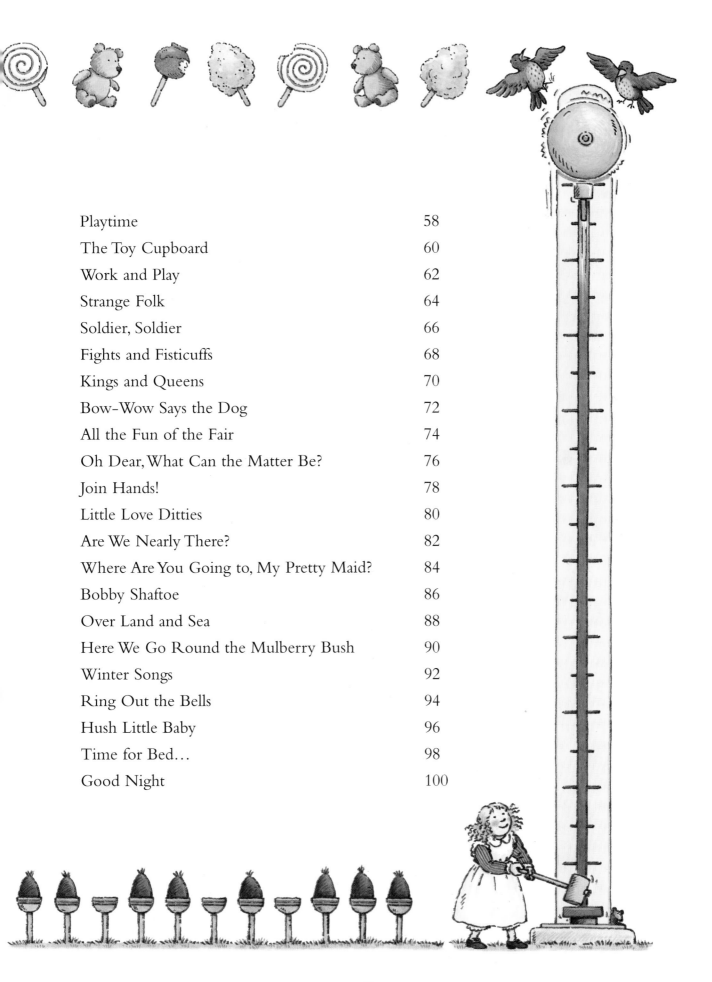

Let's Begin

Out goes the rat,
Out goes the cat,
Out goes the lady
With the big green hat.
Y, O, U, spells you;
O, U, T, spells out!

Eenie, meenie, minie, mo,
Catch a tiger by the toe,
If he hollers, let him go,
Eenie, meenie, minie, mo.

START

OUT

14

One potato, two potato,
Three potato, four;
Five potato, six potato,
Seven potato, MORE.

Dip dip dip,
My blue ship,
Sailing on the water,
Like a cup and saucer.
Dip dip dip,
You're not It.

Ickle ockle, blue bockle,
Fishes in the sea,
If you want a pretty maid,
Please choose me.

15

One to Ten, and Then Again

One, two, three,
I love coffee,
And Billy loves tea,
How good you be,
One, two, three,
I love coffee,
And Billy loves tea.

One, two, three, four, five,
Once I caught a fish alive,
Six, seven, eight, nine, ten,
Then I let it go again.
Why did you let it go?
Because it bit my finger so.
Which finger did it bite?
The little finger on the right.

16

One, two,
  Buckle my shoe;
Three, four,
  Knock at the door;
Five, six,
  Pick up sticks;
Seven, eight,
  Lay them straight;
Nine, ten,
  A big fat hen;
Eleven, twelve,
  Dig and delve;
Thirteen, fourteen,
  Maids a-courting;
Fifteen, sixteen,
  Maids in the kitchen;
Seventeen, eighteen,
  Maids in waiting;
Nineteen, twenty,
  My plate's empty.

Nursery Days

Bye, baby bunting,
Daddy's gone a-hunting,
Gone to get a rabbit skin
To wrap the baby bunting in.

Pat-a-cake, pat-a-cake, baker's man,
Bake me a cake as fast as you can;
Pat it and prick it, and mark it with B,
Put it in the oven for Baby and me.

Dance to your daddy,
   My little babby,
Dance to your daddy,
   My little lamb.

You shall have a fishy
   In a little dishy,
You shall have a fishy
   When the boat comes in.

You shall have an apple,
   You shall have a plum,
You shall have a rattle-basket
   When your daddy comes home.

Hush-a-bye, baby, on the tree top,
When the wind blows, the cradle will rock;
When the bough breaks, the cradle will fall,
And down will come baby, cradle and all.

How many days has my baby to play?
Saturday, Sunday, Monday,
Tuesday, Wednesday, Thursday, Friday,
Saturday, Sunday, Monday.
    Hop away, skip away,
    My baby wants to play;
My baby wants to play every day!

Baby Games

This little piggy went to market;
This little piggy stayed at home;
This little piggy had roast beef;
This little piggy had none;
This little piggy cried, Wee, wee, wee,
　　All the way home.

Tickly, tickly, on your knee,
If you laugh you don't love me.

Round and round the garden,
Like a teddy bear;
One step, two step,
Tickle you under there!

Clap hands, Daddy comes
With his pocket full of plums,
    And a cake for *you*.

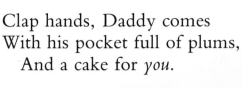

This is the way the ladies ride,
    Nim, nim, nim, nim.
This is the way the gentlemen ride,
    Trim, trim, trim, trim.
This is the way the farmers ride,
    Trot, trot, trot, trot.
This is the way the huntsmen ride,
    A-gallop, a-gallop, a-gallop.
This is the way the ploughboys ride,
    Hobble-dy-hoy, hobble-dy-hoy.

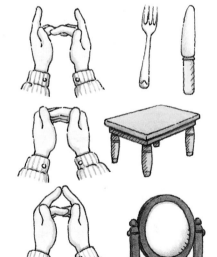

Here are the lady's knives and forks,
Here is the lady's table,
Here is the lady's looking-glass,
And here is the baby's cradle.

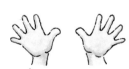

I Love Little Pussy

Puss cat Mole jumped over a coal,
And in her best petticoat burned a great hole.
Poor pussy's weeping, she'll have no more milk,
Until her best petticoat's mended with silk.

I love little pussy,
　　Her coat is so warm,
And if I don't hurt her
　　She'll do me no harm.
So I'll not pull her tail,
　　Nor drive her away,
But pussy and I
　　Very gently will play.
She shall sit by my side,
　　And I'll give her some food;
And pussy will love me
　　Because I am good.

Sing, sing,
　　What shall I sing?
The cat's run away
　　With the pudding string!
Do, do,
　　What shall I do?
The cat's run away
　　With the pudding too!

Pussy cat ate the dumplings,
Pussy cat ate the dumplings,
    Mamma stood by,
    And cried, Oh, fie!
Why did you eat the dumplings?

Who's that ringing at my door bell?
    A little pussy cat that isn't very well.
Rub its little nose with a little mutton fat,
    That's the best cure for a little pussy cat.

Ding, dong, bell,
Pussy's in the well.
Who put her in?
Little Johnny Green.
Who pulled her out?
Little Tommy Stout.
What a naughty boy was that
To try to drown poor pussy cat,
Who never did him any harm,
And killed the mice in his father's barn.

Mice Galore

Three blind mice, see how they run!
They all ran after the farmer's wife,
Who cut off their tails with a carving knife,
Did you ever see such a thing in your life,
 As three blind mice?

Three young rats with black felt hats,
Three young ducks with white straw flats,

Three young dogs with curling tails,
Three young cats with demi-veils,

Went out to walk with two young pigs
In satin vests and sorrel wigs;

But suddenly it chanced to rain
And so they all went home again.

Hickory, dickory, dock,
The mouse ran up the clock.
   The clock struck one,
   The mouse ran down,
Hickory, dickory, dock.

Six little mice sat down to spin;
Pussy passed by and she peeped in.
What are you doing, my little men?
Weaving coats for gentlemen.
Shall I come in and cut off your threads?
No, no, Mistress Pussy,
You'd bite off our heads.
Oh, no, I'll not; I'll help you to spin.
That may be so, but you don't come in.

WANTED

Sing a Song of Sixpence

Sing a song of sixpence,
A pocket full of rye;
Four and twenty blackbirds,
Baked in a pie.

When the pie was opened,
The birds began to sing;
Wasn't that a dainty dish,
To set before the king?

The king was in his counting-house,
　　Counting out his money;
The queen was in the parlour,
　　Eating bread and honey.

The maid was in the garden,
　　Hanging out the clothes,
When down came a blackbird
And pecked off her nose.

Birds of the Air

A wise old owl sat in an oak,
The more he heard the less he spoke;
The less he spoke the more he heard.
Why aren't we all like that wise old bird?

Jenny Wren fell sick
Upon a merry time,
In came Robin Redbreast
And brought her sops and wine.

Eat well of the sop, Jenny,
Drink well of the wine.
Thank you, Robin, kindly,
You shall be mine.

Jenny Wren got well,
And stood upon her feet,
And told Robin plainly,
She loved him not a bit.

Robin he got angry,
And hopped upon a twig,
Saying, Out upon you, fie upon you,
Bold faced jig!

Little Poll Parrot
Sat in his garret
Eating toast and tea;
A little brown mouse
Jumped into the house,
And stole it all away.

Little Robin Redbreast
Came to visit me;
This is what he whistled,
Thank you for my tea.

Pit, pat, well-a-day,
Little Robin flew away.
Where can little Robin be?
Gone into the cherry tree.

There were two birds sat on a stone,
　Fa, la, la, la, lal, de;
One flew away, and then there was one,
　Fa, la, la, la, lal, de;
The other flew after, and then there was none,
　Fa, la, la, la, lal, de;
And so the poor stone was left all alone,
　Fa, la, la, la, lal, de.

I Saw a Ship a-Sailing

I saw a ship a-sailing,
A-sailing on the sea,
And oh, but it was laden
With pretty things for thee!

There were comfits in the cabin,
And apples in the hold;
The sails were made of silk,
And the masts were all of gold.

The four-and-twenty sailors,
That stood between the decks,
Were four-and-twenty white mice
With chains about their necks.

The captain was a duck
With a packet on his back,
And when the ship began to move
The captain said, Quack! Quack!

The House that Jack Built

This is the house that Jack built.

This is the malt
That lay in the house
that Jack built.

This is the rat,
That ate the malt
That lay in the house
that Jack built.

This is the cat,
That killed the rat,
That ate the malt
That lay in the house
that Jack built.

This is the dog,
That worried the cat,
That killed the rat,
That ate the malt
That lay in the house
that Jack built.

This is the cow with the crumpled horn,
That tossed the dog,
That worried the cat,
That killed the rat,
That ate the malt
That lay in the house
that Jack built.

This is the maiden all forlorn,
That milked the cow with the crumpled horn,
That tossed the dog,
That worried the cat,
That killed the rat,
That ate the malt
That lay in the house
that Jack built.

This is the man all tattered and torn,
That kissed the maiden all forlorn,
That milked the cow
with the crumpled horn,
That tossed the dog,
That worried the cat,
That killed the rat,
That ate the malt
That lay in the house
that Jack built.

This is the priest all shaven and shorn,
That married the man all tattered and torn,
That kissed the maiden all forlorn,
That milked the cow with the crumpled horn,
That tossed the dog,
That worried the cat,
That killed the rat,
That ate the malt
That lay in the house
that Jack built.

This is the cock that crowed in the morn,
That waked the priest all shaven and shorn,
That married the man all tattered and torn,
That kissed the maiden all forlorn,
That milked the cow with the crumpled horn,
That tossed the dog,
That worried the cat,
That killed the rat,
That ate the malt
That lay in the house
that Jack built.

Nonsensical Rhymes

Hey diddle, diddle,
The cat and the fiddle,
The cow jumped over the moon;
The little dog laughed
To see such sport,
And the dish ran away with
the spoon.

Hoddley, poddley, puddle and fogs,
Cats are to marry the poodle dogs;
Cats in blue jackets and dogs in red hats,
What will become of the mice and the rats?

Humpty Dumpty sat on a wall,
Humpty Dumpty had a great fall;
All the King's horses
And all the King's men
Couldn't put Humpty together again.

Rub-a-dub-dub,
Three men in a tub,
And how do you think they got there?
The butcher, the baker,
The candlestick-maker,
They all jumped out of a rotten potato,
'Twas enough to make a man stare.

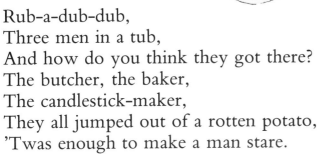

Owen Moore went away,
Owing more than he could pay.
Owen Moore came back next day,
Owing more.

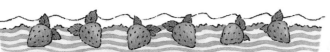

A man in the wilderness, he asked me,
How many strawberries grow in the sea?
I answered him, as I thought good,
As many red herrings as swim in the wood.

Mother, may I go out to swim?
    Yes, my darling daughter.
Hang your clothes on a hickory limb
    And don't go near the water.

In the City, In the Street

London Bridge is falling down,
Falling down, falling down;
London Bridge is falling down,
My fair lady.

We must build it up again,
Up again, up again;
We must build it up again,
My fair lady.

Up and down the City Road,
In and out the Eagle,
That's the way the money goes,
Pop goes the weasel!

Half a pound of tuppenny rice,
Half a pound of treacle,
Mix it up and make it nice,
Pop goes the weasel!

Every night when I go out
The monkey's on the table;
Take a stick and knock it off,
Pop goes the weasel!

36

Sally go round the sun,
Sally go round the moon,
Sally go round the chimney-pots
On a Saturday afternoon.

Oranges and lemons,
    Say the bells of St Clement's.
You owe me five farthings,
    Say the bells of St Martin's.
When will you pay me?
    Say the bells of Old Bailey.
When I grow rich,
    Say the bells of Shoreditch.
When will that be?
    Say the bells of Stepney.
I'm sure I don't know,
    Says the Great Bell of Bow.

Mary Had a Little Lamb

Mary had a little lamb,
  Its fleece was white as snow;
And everywhere that Mary went
  The lamb was sure to go.

It followed her to school one day,
  That was against the rule;
It made the children laugh and play
  To see a lamb at school.

And so the teacher turned it out,
But still it lingered near,
And waited patiently about
Till Mary did appear.

Why does the lamb love Mary so?
The eager children cry;
Why, Mary loves the lamb, you know,
The teacher did reply.

Down on the Farm

Come, butter, come,
Come, butter, come,
Peter stands at the gate
Waiting for a butter cake.
Come, butter, come.

Little Bo-peep has lost her sheep,
And doesn't know where to find them;
Leave them alone, and they'll come home,
Bringing their tails behind them.

If I had a donkey that wouldn't go,
Would I beat him? Oh no, no.
I'd put him in the barn and give him some corn,
The best little donkey that ever was born.

Baa, baa, black sheep,
  Have you any wool?
Yes, sir, yes, sir,
  Three bags full;
One for the master,
  And one for the dame,
And one for the little boy
  Who lives down the lane.

Going for a Ride

Yankee Doodle came to town,
Riding on a pony;
He stuck a feather in his cap
And called it macaroni.

I had a little pony,
His name was Dapple Gray;
I lent him to a lady
To ride a mile away.
She whipped him, she lashed him,
She rode him through the mire,
I would not lend my pony now,
For all the lady's hire.

Ride a cock-horse to Banbury Cross,
To see a fine lady upon a white horse;
Rings on her fingers and bells on her toes,
She shall have music wherever she goes.

Shoe a little horse,
Shoe a little mare,
But let the little colt
Go bare, bare, bare.

A farmer went trotting upon his grey mare,
   Bumpety, bumpety, bump!
With his daughter behind him so rosy and fair,
   Lumpety, lumpety, lump!

A raven cried, Croak! and they all tumbled down,
   Bumpety, bumpety, bump!
The mare broke her knees and the farmer his crown,
   Lumpety, lumpety, lump!

The mischievous raven flew laughing away,
   Bumpety, bumpety, bump!
And vowed he would serve them the same the next day,
   Lumpety, lumpety, lump!

Cherry Stone Rhymes

Who shall I marry?

Tinker,
Tailor,
Soldier,
Sailor,
Rich man,
Poor man,
Beggar man,
Thief.

When will it be?

This year,
Next year,
Sometime,
Never.

Where shall I marry?

Church,
Chapel,
Cathedral,
Abbey.

And the ring?

Gold,
Silver,
Copper,
Brass.

How shall I get there?

Coach,
Carriage,
Wheelbarrow,
Dustcart.

What shall I wear?

Silk,
Satin,
Cotton,
Rags.

And where shall we live happily ever after?

Big house,
Little house,
Pig sty,
Barn.

What's for Dinner?

Polly put the kettle on,
Polly put the kettle on,
Polly put the kettle on,
　We'll all have tea.

Sukey take it off again,
Sukey take it off again,
Sukey take it off again,
　They've all gone away.

Davy Davy Dumpling,
　Boil him in the pot;
Sugar him and butter him,
　And eat him while he's hot.

Little Tommy Tucker
　Sings for his supper:
What shall we give him?
　White bread and butter.
How shall he cut it
　Without e'er a knife?
How will he be married
　Without e'er a wife?

Little Miss Muffet
Sat on a tuffet,
Eating her curds and whey;
There came a big spider,
Who sat down beside her
And frightened Miss Muffet away.

Pease porridge hot,
Pease porridge cold,
Pease porridge in the pot
Nine days old.
Some like it hot,
Some like it cold,
Some like it in the pot
Nine days old.

Jack Sprat could eat no fat,
    His wife could eat no lean,
And so between them both, you see,
    They licked the platter clean.

Bad Boys and Naughty Girls

Diddle, diddle, dumpling, my son John,
Went to bed with his trousers on;
One shoe off, and one shoe on,
Diddle, diddle, dumpling, my son John.

There was a little girl, and she had a little curl
Right in the middle of her forehead;
When she was good she was very, very good,
But when she was bad she was horrid.

Georgie Porgie, pudding and pie,
Kissed the girls and made them cry;
When the boys came out to play,
Georgie Porgie ran away.

Elsie Marley is grown so fine,
She won't get up to feed the swine,
But lies in bed till eight or nine.
    Lazy Elsie Marley.

Little Tommy Tittlemouse
Lived in a little house;
He caught fishes
In other men's ditches.

Handy Pandy Jack-a-Dandy
Stole a piece of sugar candy
From the grocer's shoppy-shop,
And away did hoppy-hop.

Little Polly Flinders
Sat among the cinders,
Warming her pretty little toes;
Her mother came and caught her,
And whipped her little daughter
For spoiling her nice new clothes.

49

Jack and Jill

Jack and Jill
Went up the hill,
To fetch a pail of water;
Jack fell down,
And broke his crown,
And Jill came tumbling after.

Then up Jack got,
And home did trot,
As fast as he could caper;
He went to bed,
To mend his head,
With vinegar and brown paper.

51

Pigs to Market

To market, to market, to buy a fat pig,
Home again, home again, jiggety jig;
To market, to market, to buy a fat hog,
Home again, home again, jiggety jog.

Tom, Tom, the piper's son,
Stole a pig and away he run;
The pig was eat,
And Tom was beat,
And Tom went howling down the street.

Dickery, dickery, dare,
The pig flew up in the air;
The man in brown
Soon brought him down
Dickery, dickery, dare.

Higglety, pigglety, pop!
The dog has eaten the mop;
The pig's in a hurry,
The cat's in a flurry,
Higglety, pigglety, pop!

Rain, Rain, Go Away!

Blow, wind, blow!
And go, mill, go!
That the miller may grind his corn;
That the baker may take it,
And into bread make it,
And bring us a loaf in the morn.

March winds and April showers
Bring forth May flowers.

Rain, rain, go away,
Come again another day,
Little Johnny wants to play.

Ipsey Wipsey spider
   Climbing up the spout;
Down came the rain
   And washed the spider out:
Out came the sunshine
   And dried up all the rain;
Ipsey Wipsey spider
   Climbing up again.

A sunshiny shower
Won't last half an hour.

Rain on the green grass,
   And rain on the tree,
Rain on the house-top,
   But not on me.

Lazy Days

Buttercups and daisies,
Oh what pretty flowers
Coming in the springtime
To tell of sunny hours.
While the trees are leafless,
While the fields are bare,
Buttercups and daisies
Spring up everywhere.

A diller, a dollar,
A ten o'clock scholar,
What makes you come so soon?
You used to come at ten o'clock,
But now you come at noon.

Ladybird, ladybird,
Fly away home,
Your house is on fire
And your children are gone;
All except one
And that's little Ann
And she has crept under
The frying pan.

The cock's on the wood pile
   Blowing his horn,
The bull's in the barn
   A-threshing the corn,
The maids in the meadow
   Are making the hay,
The ducks in the river
   Are swimming away.

A swarm of bees in May
Is worth a load of hay;
A swarm of bees in June
Is worth a silver spoon;
A swarm of bees in July
Is not worth a fly.

Little Boy Blue,
   Come blow your horn,
The sheep's in the meadow,
   The cow's in the corn.
Where is the boy
   Who looks after the sheep?
He's under a haycock
   Fast asleep.
Will you wake him?
   No, not I,
For if I do,
   He's sure to cry.

Playtime

I'm the king of the castle,
Get down you dirty rascal.

I'll sing you a song,
Nine verses long,
  For a pin;
Three and three are six,
And three are nine;
You are a fool,
  And the pin is mine.

Tell tale tit,
Your tongue shall be split
And all the little puppy dogs,
Shall have a little bit!

58

Finders keepers,
Losers weepers.

Here am I,
  Little Jumping Joan;
When nobody's with me
  I'm all alone.

Lucy Locket lost her pocket,
  Kitty Fisher found it;
Not a penny was there in it,
  Only ribbon round it.

The Toy Cupboard

Little John Jiggy Jag,
He rode a penny nag,
  And went to Wigan to woo:
When he came to a beck,
He fell and broke his neck,
  Johnny, how dost thou now?

I made him a hat
Of my coat lap,
  And stockings of pearly blue;
A hat and a feather,
To keep out cold weather,
  So, Johnny, how dost thou now?

Jerry Hall,
  He is so small,
  A rat could eat him,
Hat and all.

I had a little moppet,
I kept it in my pocket
And fed it on corn and hay;
There came a proud beggar
And said he would wed her,
And stole my little moppet away.

Hush baby, my doll, I pray you don't cry,
And I'll give you some bread and some milk by and
    by;
Or, perhaps you like custard, or may be a tart,
Then to either you're welcome, with all my whole
    heart.

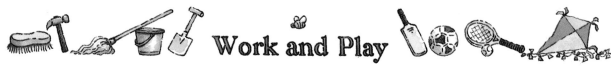

Work and Play

My maid Mary,
She minds the dairy,
While I go a-hoeing and mowing
    each morn;
Merrily runs the reel,
And the little spinning wheel,
Whilst I am singing and mowing
    my corn.

Cobbler, cobbler, mend my shoe,
Get it done by half past two;
Stitch it up, and stitch it down,
And I will give you half a crown.

Can you wash your father's shirt,
    Can you wash it clean?
Can you wash your father's shirt
    And bleach it on the green?
Yes, I can wash my father's shirt,
    And I can wash it clean.
I can wash my father's shirt
    And send it to the Queen.

Meadowsweet,
And thistledown,
Up the hill,
And tumble down.

There was a jolly miller once,
  Lived on the river Dee;
He worked and sang from morn till night,
  No lark so blithe as he.
And this the burden of his song
  For ever used to be,
I care for nobody – no! not I
  If nobody cares for me.

Wash the dishes, wipe the dishes,
  Ring the bell for tea;
Three good wishes, three good
    kisses,
  I will give to thee.

See-saw, Margery Daw,
Jacky shall have a new master;
Jacky shall have but a penny a day,
Because he can't work any faster.

Strange Folk

Goosey, goosey gander,
   Whither shall I wander?
Upstairs and downstairs
   And in my lady's chamber.
There I met an old man
   Who would not say his prayers,
I took him by the left leg
   And threw him down the stairs.

Peter, Peter, pumpkin eater,
Had a wife and couldn't keep her;
He put her in a pumpkin shell
And there he kept her very well.

Peter, Peter, pumpkin eater,
Had another, and didn't love her;
Peter learned to read and spell,
And then he loved her very well.

Mrs. Mason bought a basin,
Mrs. Tyson said, What a nice 'un,
What did it cost? said Mrs. Frost,
Half a crown, said Mrs. Brown,
Did it indeed, said Mrs. Reed,
It did for certain, said Mrs. Burton.
Then Mrs. Nix up to her tricks
Threw the basin on the bricks.

There was an old woman tossed up in a basket,
Seventeen times as high as the moon;
Where she was going I couldn't but ask it,
For in her hand she carried a broom.
Old woman, old woman, old woman, quoth I,
Where are you going to up so high?
To brush the cobwebs off the sky!
May I go with you? Aye, by-and-by.

There was a crooked man
    And he walked a crooked mile;
He found a crooked sixpence
    Against a crooked stile;
He bought a crooked cat
    Which caught a crooked mouse,
And they all lived together
    In a little crooked house.

Doctor Foster went to Gloucester
In a shower of rain;
He stepped in a puddle,
Right up to his middle,
And never went there again.

Soldier, Soldier

Oh, soldier, soldier, will you marry me,
  With your musket, fife, and drum?
Oh no, pretty maid, I cannot marry you,
  For I have no coat to put on.

Then away she went
  To her grandfather's chest,
And brought him one of the very very best,
  And the soldier put it on.

Oh, soldier, soldier, will you marry me,
  With your musket, fife, and drum?
Oh no, pretty maid, I cannot marry you,
  For I have no socks to put on.

Then away she went
  To her grandfather's chest,
And brought him a pair of the very very best,
  And the soldier put them on.

Oh, soldier, soldier, will you marry me,
    With your musket, fife, and drum?
Oh no, pretty maid, I cannot marry you
    For I have no shoes to put on.

Then away she went
    To her grandfather's chest,
And brought him a pair of the very very best,
    And the soldier put them on.

Oh, soldier, soldier, will you marry me,
    With your musket, fife, and drum?
Oh no, pretty maid, I cannot marry you,
    For I have no hat to put on.

Then away she went
    To her grandfather's chest,
And brought him one of the very very best,
    And the soldier put it on.

Oh, soldier, soldier, will you marry me,
    With your musket, fife, and drum?
Oh no, pretty maid, I cannot marry you,
    For I have a wife at home.

Fights and Fisticuffs

The lion and the unicorn
　　Were fighting for the crown;
The lion beat the unicorn
　　All around the town.

Some gave them white bread,
　　And some gave them brown;
Some gave them plum cake
　　And drummed them out of town.

Tweedledum and Tweedledee
　　Agreed to have a battle,
For Tweedledum said Tweedledee
　　Had spoiled his nice new rattle.
Just then flew by a monstrous crow
　　As big as a tar-barrel,
Which frightened both the heroes so,
　　They quite forgot their quarrel.

Oh, the grand old Duke of York,
He had ten thousand men;
He marched them up
To the top of the hill,
And he marched them down again.

And when they were up, they were up,
And when they were down, they were down,
And when they were only half-way up,
They were neither up nor down.

Punch and Judy
    Fought for a pie;
Punch gave Judy
    A knock in the eye.
Says Punch to Judy,
    Will you have any more?
Says Judy to Punch,
    My eye is too sore.

Kings and Queens

Old King Cole
Was a merry old soul,
And a merry old soul was he;
He called for his pipe,
And he called for his bowl,
And he called for his fiddlers three.

Every fiddler he had a fiddle,
And a very fine fiddle had he
Oh, there's none so rare
As can compare
With King Cole and his fiddlers
three.

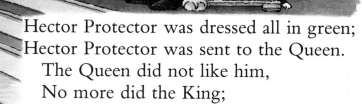

Hector Protector was dressed all in green;
Hector Protector was sent to the Queen.
The Queen did not like him,
No more did the King;
So Hector Protector was sent back again.

Lavender's blue, diddle, diddle,
Lavender's green;
When I am king, diddle, diddle,
You shall be queen.

I had a little nut tree,
Nothing would it bear
But a silver nutmeg
And a golden pear;
The king of Spain's daughter
Came to visit me,
And all for the sake
Of my little nut tree.
I skipped over water,
I danced over sea,
And all the birds in the air
Couldn't catch me.

The Queen of Hearts
She made some tarts,
All on a summer's day;
The Knave of Hearts
He stole those tarts,
And took them clean away.

The King of Hearts
Called for the tarts,
And beat the knave full sore;
The Knave of Hearts
Brought back the tarts,
And vowed he'd steal no more.

Bow-Wow Says the Dog

I had a dog
    Whose name was Buff,
I sent him for
    A bag of snuff;
He broke the bag
    And spilled the stuff,
And that was all
    My penny's worth.

Old Mother Hubbard
Went to the cupboard,
To fetch her poor dog a bone.
When she got there,
The cupboard was bare,
And so the poor dog had none.

72

I had a dog and his name was Dandy,
His tail was long and his legs were bandy,
His eyes were brown and his coat was sandy,
The best in the world was my dog Dandy.

Oh where, oh where has my little dog gone?
Oh where, oh where can he be?
With his ears cut short and his tail cut long,
Oh where, oh where is he?

Hark, hark,
    The dogs do bark,
The beggars are coming to town;
    Some in rags,
    And some in jags,
And one in a velvet gown.

All the Fun of the Fair

Smiling girls, rosy boys,
Come and buy my little toys;
Monkeys made of gingerbread,
And sugar horses painted red.

As I was going to Banbury,
  Upon a summer's day,
My dame had butter, eggs, and fruit,
  And I had corn and hay.
Joe drove the ox, and Tom the swine,
  Dick took the foal and mare;
I sold them all, then home to dine,
  From famous Banbury fair.

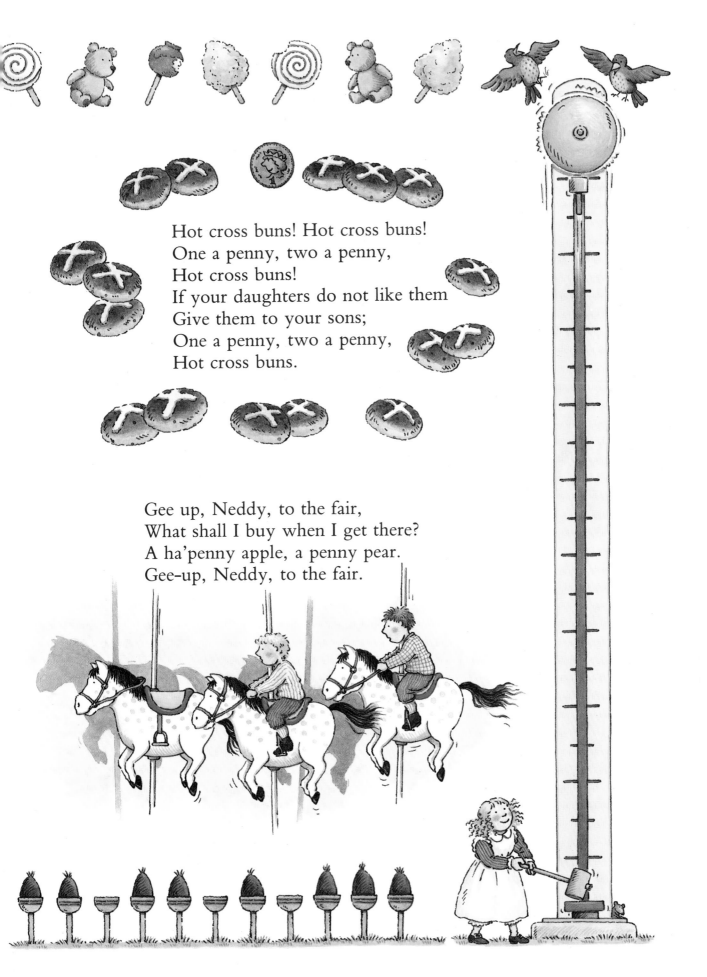

Hot cross buns! Hot cross buns!
One a penny, two a penny,
Hot cross buns!
If your daughters do not like them
Give them to your sons;
One a penny, two a penny,
Hot cross buns.

Gee up, Neddy, to the fair,
What shall I buy when I get there?
A ha'penny apple, a penny pear.
Gee-up, Neddy, to the fair.

Oh Dear, What Can the Matter Be?

Oh, dear, what can the matter be?
Dear, dear, what can the matter be?
Oh, dear, what can the matter be?
Johnny's so long at the fair.

He promised he'd buy me a fairing should please me,
And then for a kiss, oh! he vowed he would tease me,
He promised he'd bring me a bunch of blue ribbons
To tie up my bonny brown hair.

Oh, dear, what can the matter be?
Dear, dear, what can the matter be?
Oh, dear, what can the matter be?
Johnny's so long at the fair.

He promised he'd bring me a basket of posies,
A garland of lilies, a garland of roses,
A little straw hat, to set off the blue ribbons
That tie up my bonny brown hair.

Oh, dear, what can the matter be?
Dear, dear, what can the matter be?
Oh, dear, what can the matter be?
Johnny's so long at the fair.

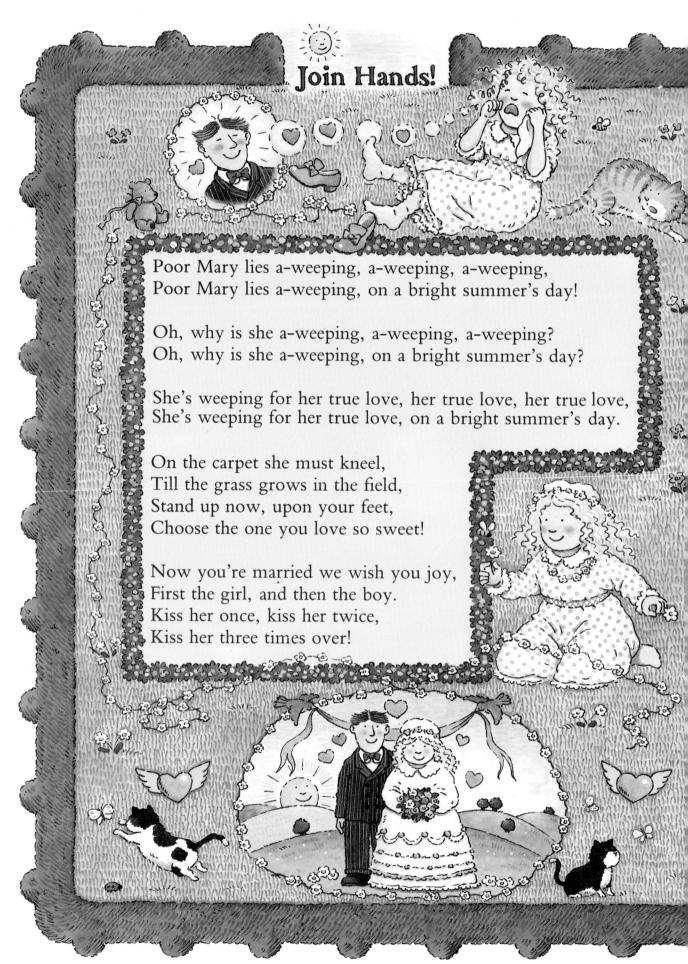

Join Hands!

Poor Mary lies a-weeping, a-weeping, a-weeping,
Poor Mary lies a-weeping, on a bright summer's day!

Oh, why is she a-weeping, a-weeping, a-weeping?
Oh, why is she a-weeping, on a bright summer's day?

She's weeping for her true love, her true love, her true love,
She's weeping for her true love, on a bright summer's day.

On the carpet she must kneel,
Till the grass grows in the field,
Stand up now, upon your feet,
Choose the one you love so sweet!

Now you're married we wish you joy,
First the girl, and then the boy.
Kiss her once, kiss her twice,
Kiss her three times over!

Ring-a-ring o'roses,
A pocket full of posies,
 A-tishoo! A-tishoo!
We all fall down.

The cows are in the meadow
Lying fast asleep,
 A-tishoo! A-tishoo!
We all get up again.

Little Love Ditties

Curly locks, Curly locks,
  Wilt thou be mine?
Thou shalt not wash dishes
  Nor yet feed the swine;
But sit on a cushion
  And sew a fine seam,
And feed upon strawberries,
  Sugar and cream.

INGREDIENTS
IN

What are little boys made of?
What are little boys made of?
  Frogs and snails
  And puppy-dogs' tails,
That's what little boys are made of.

What are little girls made of?
What are little girls made of?
  Sugar and spice
  And all things nice,
That's what little girls are made of.

BOY GIRL

OUT

OUT

One I love,
Two I love,
Three I love, I say,
Four I love with all my heart,
Five I cast away;
Six he loves me,
Seven he don't,
Eight we're lovers both;
Nine he comes,
Ten he tarries,
Eleven he courts,
Twelve he marries.

He loves me,
He don't,
He'll have me,
He won't
He would
If he could,
But he can't,
So he don't.

She loves me,
She loves me not,
She loves me,
She loves me not,
She loves me!

Roses are red,
Violets are blue,
Sugar is sweet
And so are you.

Are We Nearly There?

How many miles to Babylon?
Three-score and ten.
Can I get there by candle-light?
Yes, and back again.
If your heels are nimble and light,
You may get there by candle-light.

See-saw, sacradown,
Which is the way to London town?
One foot up and the other foot down,
That is the way to London town.

The man in the moon
Came down too soon,
And asked his way to Norwich;
He went by the south,
And burned his mouth
With supping cold plum porridge.

Three wise men of Gotham
Went to sea in a bowl;
If the bowl had been stronger,
My tale would have been longer.

Where Are You Going to, My Pretty Maid?

Where are you going to, my pretty maid?
I'm going a-milking, sir, she said,
Sir, she said, sir, she said,
I'm going a-milking, sir, she said.

May I go with you, my pretty maid?
You're kindly welcome, sir, she said,
Sir, she said, sir, she said,
You're kindly welcome, sir, she said.

Say, will you marry me, my pretty maid?
Yes, if you please, kind sir, she said,
Sir, she said, sir, she said,
Yes, if you please, kind sir, she said.

What is your father, my pretty maid?
My father's a farmer, sir, she said,
Sir, she said, sir, she said,
My father's a farmer, sir, she said.

What is your fortune, my pretty maid?
My face is my fortune, sir, she said,
Sir, she said, sir, she said,
My face is my fortune, sir, she said.

Then I can't marry you, my pretty maid.
Nobody asked you, sir, she said,
Sir, she said, sir, she said,
Nobody asked you, sir, she said.

Bobby Shaftoe

Bobby Shaftoe's gone to sea,
Silver buckles at his knee;
He'll come back and marry me,
Bonny Bobby Shaftoe.

Bobby Shaftoe's bright and fair,
Combing down his yellow hair,
He's my ain for evermair,
Bonny Bobby Shaftoe.

Bobby Shaftoe's tall and slim,
He's always dressed so neat and trim,
The ladies they all keek at him,
Bonny Bobby Shaftoe.

Bobby Shaftoe's getten a bairn
For to dandle in his arm;
In his arm and on his knee,
Bobby Shaftoe loves me.

Over Land and Sea

Over the water and over the lea,
And over the water to Charlie.
I'll have none of your nasty beef,
Nor I'll have none of your barley,
But I'll have some of your very best flour
To make a white cake for my Charlie.

My mother sent me for some water,
For some water from the sea,
My foot slipped, and in I tumbled,
Three jolly sailors came to me:
One said he'd buy me silks and satins,
One said he'd buy me a guinea gold ring,
One said he'd buy me a silver cradle
For to rock my baby in.

If all the world was paper,
　And all the sea was ink,
If all the trees were bread and cheese,
　What should we have to drink?

Little Tee Wee,
He went to sea
In an open boat:
And while afloat
The little boat bended,
And my story's ended.

If all the seas were one sea,
　What a great sea that would be!
If all the trees were one tree,
　What a great tree that would be!
And if all the axes were one axe,
　What a great axe that would be!
And if all the men were one man,
　What a great man that would be!
And if the great man took the great axe,
　And cut down the great tree,
And let it fall into the great sea,
　What a splish-splash *that* would be!

89

Here We Go Round the Mulberry Bush

Here we go round the mulberry bush,
The mulberry bush, the mulberry bush,
Here we go round the mulberry bush,
On a cold and frosty morning.

This is the way we wash our hands,
Wash our hands, wash our hands,
This is the way we wash our hands,
On a cold and frosty morning.

This is the way we wash our clothes,
Wash our clothes, wash our clothes,
This is the way we wash our clothes,
On a cold and frosty morning.

This is the way we go to school,
Go to school, go to school,
This is the way we go to school,
On a cold and frosty morning.

This is the way we come out of school,
Come out of school, come out of school,
This is the way we come out of school,
On a cold and frosty morning.

Winter Songs

The north wind doth blow,
And we shall have snow,
And what will poor Robin do then?
    Poor thing.
He'll sit in a barn,
And keep himself warm,
And hide his head under his wing,
    Poor thing.

Cuckoo, cuckoo, cherry tree,
Catch a bird, and give it me;
Let the tree be high or low,
Let it hail or rain or snow.

Button to chin
When October comes in.
Cast not a clout
Till May be out.

Snow, snow faster,
Ally-ally-blaster;
The old woman's plucking her geese,
Selling the feathers a penny a piece.

Jingle bells! Jingle bells!
Jingle all the way:
Oh, what fun it is to ride
In a one-horse open sleigh.

93

Ring Out the Bells

Christmas is coming,
    The geese are getting fat,
Please put a penny
    In the old man's hat.
If you haven't got a penny,
    A ha'penny will do;
If you haven't got a ha'penny,
    Then God bless you!

Little Jack Horner
Sat in the corner,
Eating a Christmas pie;
He put in his thumb,
And pulled out a plum,
And said, What a good boy am I!

94

Merry are the bells, and merry would they ring,
Merry was myself, and merry could I sing;
With a merry ding-dong, happy, gay, and free,
And a merry sing-song, happy let us be.

God bless the master of this house,
  And its good mistress too,
And all the little children
  That round the table go;
And all your kin and kinsmen,
  That dwell both far and near;
We wish you a merry Christmas
  And a happy New Year.

Hush Little Baby

Hush, little baby, don't say a word,
Papa's going to buy you a mocking bird.

If the mocking bird won't sing,
Papa's going to buy you a diamond ring.

If the diamond ring turns to brass,
Papa's going to buy you a looking-glass.

If the looking-glass gets broke,
Papa's going to buy you a billy-goat.

If that billy-goat runs away,
Papa's going to buy you another today.

Boys and girls come out to play,
The moon doth shine as bright as day.
Leave your supper and leave your sleep,
And join your playfellows in the street.
Come with a whoop and come with a call,
Come with a good will or not at all.
Up the ladder and down the wall,
A half-penny loaf will serve us all;
You find milk, and I'll find flour,
And we'll have a pudding in half an hour.

Jack be nimble,
Jack be quick,
Jack jump over
The candlestick.

Twinkle, twinkle, little star,
How I wonder what you are!
Up above the world so high,
Like a diamond in the sky.

Wee Willie Winkie runs through the town,
Upstairs and downstairs in his night-gown,
Rapping at the window, crying through the lock,
Are all the children in their beds, it's now eight o'clock?

Good Night

Down with the lambs,
Up with the lark,
Run to bed children
Before it gets dark.

Good night, God bless you,
Go to bed and undress you.

Good night, sweet repose,
Half the bed and all the clothes.

Come, let's to bed,
Says Sleepy-head;
Tarry a while, says Slow;
Put on the pot,
Says Greedy-gut,
We'll sup before we go.

Rock-a-bye, baby,
    Thy cradle is green,
Father's a nobleman,
    Mother's a queen;
And Betty's a lady,
    And wears a gold ring;
And Johnny's a drummer,
    And drums for the king.

Go to bed first,
A golden purse;
Go to bed second,
A golden pheasant;
Go to bed third,
A golden bird.

THE
BEST EVER
NURSERY TALES

CONTENTS

LITTLE RED RIDING HOOD

Once upon a time, on the edge of the big wood, there lived a little girl called Little Red Riding Hood. Her real name was Brenda but she was always known as Little Red Riding Hood because this was what her mother called her when she was a baby. Brenda used to wear a red bonnet when she went out for a ride in her pram, and she still wears it now.

One day Little Red Riding Hood was playing out in the sunshine when her mother called her, "I want you to go over to Grandma's house with some groceries. Grandma's not very well and she hasn't been able to get out to the shops."

"Do I have to?" said Little Red Riding Hood with a glum face.

"Yes you do!" said Mum. "Now go and wash your face." Mum packed the groceries into a basket while Little Red Riding Hood did as she was told.

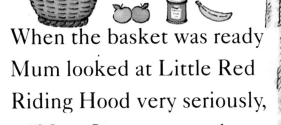

When the basket was ready
Mum looked at Little Red
Riding Hood very seriously,
"Now, I want you to be
very sensible," she said.
"Go straight through the wood
to Grandma's house. Don't
mess about. Stay on the path
and don't talk to any strangers."

She kissed Little Red Riding Hood on top of her head,
handed her the basket of groceries, and pushed her out of
the door. Little Red Riding Hood scowled and stomped
off down the path into the wood.

Little Red Riding Hood hadn't been walking far when she heard a rustling in the trees. Then she heard a deep, silky voice calling, "Little girl, little girl, can you spare a minute?"

Little Red Riding Hood was curious and strayed off the path to see where the voice was coming from. It seemed to come from the dark shadows behind the trees. There was a funny smell of old dogs and, for a moment, she thought she saw a tall woolly figure. She remembered what her mum had said but the voice was quite friendly.

"What do you want?" said Little Red Riding Hood boldly.

"Where are you going little girl?" said the voice.

"I'm going to Grandma's house. She's not well and I'm taking her some groceries," said Little Red Riding Hood.

"How kind," said the voice. "What a good girl you must be. And where does your poor grandmother live?"

Little Red Riding Hood smiled angelically and replied in her sweetest voice, "She lives at the far side of the wood, next to the pond."

"What a pleasant place to live," said the soft voice, "but you mustn't keep the old lady waiting. Off you go, dear."

Little Red Riding Hood waved and continued on to Grandma's house.

When Little Red Riding Hood was out of sight the tall woolly figure stepped out of the shadows and smiled a big sharp-toothed smile.

The silky voice belonged to a wolf!

He was hungry and wanted to eat Little Red Riding Hood but he was also clever. He was too near the little girl's house and her mother might hear her scream.

If he took the short cut through the trees, he thought, he could arrive at Grandma's house before Little Red Riding Hood, and then he could eat the tasty little girl and her fat old grandmother. Licking his lips he raced off into the dark wood.

When the wolf reached Grandma's house he sneaked around the back and peeked in through the kitchen window. Grandma was making a pot of tea. The wolf lifted the latch silently and tip-toed in when Grandma's back was turned. Then, before Grandma could shout, 'tea-bag!' the greedy wolf swallowed her whole.

"Mmm, yum, yum," he said. Then, he hurried to Grandma's bedroom and searched her drawers until he found a big pink nightgown and a frilly nightcap.

Quickly the wolf dressed himself in Grandma's clothes and leapt into bed just as he heard Little Red Riding Hood approaching the house.

"Grandma, where are you?" shouted Little Red Riding
Hood.

"I'm in bed, child," called the wolf in his best 'old lady'
voice. "Come right in, the door's not locked."

Little Red Riding Hood opened the back door and
stepped into the kitchen. There was a funny smell which
was different from Grandma's smell, and the teapot lay
broken on the floor.

"Grandma, are you all right?" called Little Red Riding
Hood.

"Yes dear, I'm not feeling myself today so I decided to
go back to bed. Do come in and see me."

It was dark in Grandma's room because the curtains were drawn. Little Red Riding Hood, still holding the basket of groceries, stood beside the bed. How strange, she thought, there was that funny smell of old dogs again. She looked at the figure under the great heap of bedclothes and frowned.

"Grandma, are you sure you're all right?" said Little Red Riding Hood.

"Of course, my child. I'm just a bit under the weather," said the wolf.

Little Red Riding Hood thought Grandma's voice
sounded strange, but she did have a bad cold. Then she
noticed Grandma's ears.

"Grandma, what big ears you have!"

"All the better to hear you with, my dear," said the wolf.

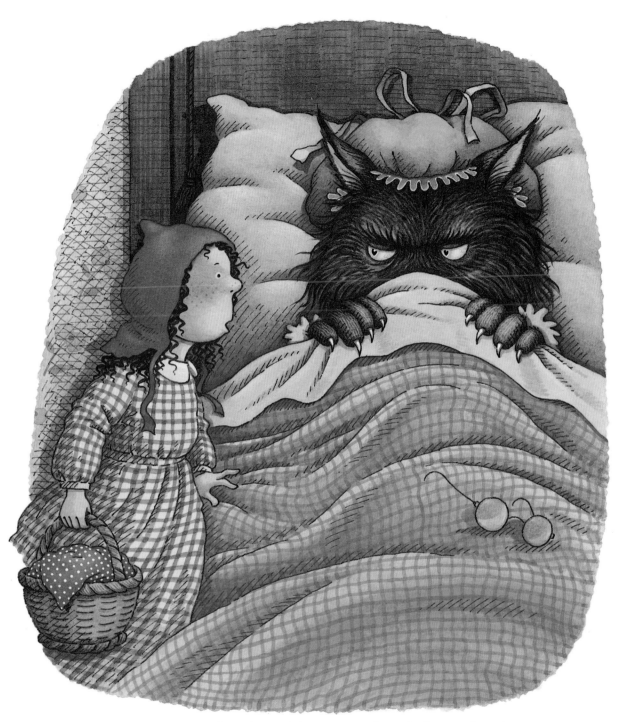

Then Little Red Riding Hood noticed Grandma's
gleaming eyes.

"Grandma, what big eyes you have!"

"All the better to see you with, my dear," said the wolf.

Then, as Little Red Riding Hood's eyes became accustomed to the dim light, she noticed Grandma's pointed nose and shining teeth.

"Grandma, what big teeth you have!"

At this the wolf leapt up and growled, "ALL THE BETTER TO EAT YOU WITH, MY DEAR!"

The wolf's jaws were all around her but, quick as a flash, Little Red Riding Hood swung the shopping basket and hit the wolf squarely on the nose. He yelped and fell back.

At that moment the door burst open and there stood Mum with Grandma's frying pan in her hand! She lifted it high above her head, then brought it down with a CLANG! on the wicked wolf's head.

He did not move again.

Little Red Riding Hood ran to her mother who hugged
her tight. "Mum, why are you here?" she said.

"I had a funny feeling in my bones," said Mum, "so I
decided to come and see how Grandma was for myself.
Where is she?"

There was a muffled cry from where the wolf was lying
and something was moving in the wolf's tummy!

"Quick, Little Red Riding Hood, get the scissors," said Mum. With a snip, snip, snip, Mum cut open the wolf's tummy and out spilled an angry Grandma. She was shaken but, luckily, not harmed in any way.

"I'm going to teach that wolf a lesson," said Grandma.
"Fetch me my sewing basket Little Red Riding Hood."

Grandma worked quickly. From under the kitchen sink
she pulled a sack of onions. She stuffed them all into the
wolf's tummy then, with her best embroidery stitches,
sewed up the woolly beast's belly.

Then Grandma, Mum and Little Red Riding Hood together rolled the sleeping wolf across the floor and out of the door. Grandma slammed the door shut.

"Put the kettle on Little Red Riding Hood, what we need now is a cup of tea," said Grandma, who was feeling much better.

When the wolf woke up he felt terrible. His head hurt and his tummy felt as though it was on fire. "Ooooh," he said to himself, "I'll never eat another grandma again."

He never did, and he never talked to strange girls again either.

THE THREE BEARS AND GOLDILOCKS

Once upon a time, there were three bears who lived in a little house in the big wood. There was a great big bear called George, a middle-sized bear called Mavis and a tiny little bear called Brian; but they were better known as Father Bear, Mother Bear and Baby Bear, or The Three Bears.

The Three Bears lived very happily and quietly together
in their house which was always tidy. They each had their
own things. They had their own food bowls: a big one
with daisies on for Father Bear, a middle-sized one with
buttercups on for Mother Bear and a little one with
rabbits on for Baby Bear.

They had their own chairs: a big one with a high back and arms for Father Bear, a middle-sized one with big cushions for Mother Bear and a little one with rabbits on for Baby Bear. They had their own beds: a big one with a carved headboard for Father Bear, a middle-sized one with a quilted headboard for Mother Bear and a little one with rabbits on for Baby Bear.

One morning, when it was his turn to make breakfast,
Father Bear made a big pot of porridge. When it was
ready, he poured it into the three bowls. It was still too
hot to eat so Father Bear suggested, as it was a sunny
morning, that they all go for a stroll in the woods while
the porridge cooled. After opening all the windows to let
the sun in to warm the house, they set off down the path.

On that same morning there was someone else walking in the big wood. A little girl called Goldilocks was stomping along swatting at butterflies with a stick and kicking the heads off flowers. She was in a bad mood. Her mum had told her off and she'd slammed out of the house without any breakfast.

Goldilocks was feeling very hungry when she suddenly smelled the warm, delicious smell of porridge. She followed the smell with her nose until she came to where The Three Bears' house stood in a sunny clearing.

Goldilocks liked the look
of the house and, when
she peeped through the open
window, she saw three bowls
of porridge on the table.
Goldilocks' empty tummy
grumbled. She wondered
if whoever lived in
the house might like to
share their breakfast
with her, so she
knocked on the door.
There was no reply.
Goldilocks then lifted
the latch to see if the
door was locked. It
wasn't. After looking
around, she opened
the door, stepped
inside, and went
straight for the
bowls of porridge
on the table.

She first tried the biggest
bowl with the most amount
of porridge in it.

"Oooh!" said Goldilocks.
"Too hot."

Then she tried the
middle-sized bowl.

"Yuk, too cold!" she said.

Next she tried the little
bowl with the rabbits on.

"Yum, yum just right," she
said, and quickly ate it all up.

Goldilocks then started to make herself at home.

She tried sitting in the biggest chair but it was very uncomfortable.

"Too hard," said Goldilocks.

Then she tried the middle-sized chair.

"Too soft," she said.

Next she tried the little chair.

"Mmm, just right," she said. She liked this one and wriggled with glee, so much so that – CRASH! – the back legs broke and she fell to the floor.

Picking herself up, and feeling a bit cross, Goldilocks then decided to explore the rest of the house. She went upstairs to the bedroom where she found the three beds.

First she tried lying on the biggest bed.

"Too high," she said.

Then she tried lying on the middle-sized bed.

"Too low," said Goldilocks.

Next she tried the little bed.

"Aaah, just right," she said.

It was so comfortable that she immediately
fell fast asleep.

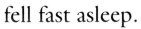

Very soon The Three Bears returned home from their walk and were surprised to find the door open. They looked inside and noticed the bowls of porridge on the table.

"Somebody has been eating my porridge!" said Father Bear in a great, gruff, growling voice.

"Somebody has been eating my porridge!" said Mother Bear in a mellow, middle-sized voice.

"Somebody has been eating my porridge, and has eaten it all up!" cried Baby Bear in a squeaky, little voice.

Then they noticed the chairs had been moved.

"Somebody has been sitting in my chair!"
said Father Bear in a great, gruff, growling voice.

"Somebody has been sitting in my chair!" said Mother Bear in a mellow, middle-sized voice.

"Somebody has been sitting in my chair, and broken it all to bits!" sobbed Baby Bear in a squeaky, little voice, dripping tears on to the floor.

The Three Bears then heard the sound of snoring coming from upstairs.

They tiptoed up the stairs and into the bedroom. They looked at the rumpled beds.

"Somebody has been lying on my bed!"
said Father Bear in a great, gruff, growling voice.

"Somebody has been lying on my bed!" said
Mother Bear in a mellow, middle-sized voice.

"Somebody has been lying on my bed, and she's still there!"
wailed Baby Bear in a squeaky, little voice.

This commotion woke Goldilocks up with a start. Seeing
The Three Bears she screamed.

"EEEEAAAWWAAAGHH!"

This so frightened The Three Bears that they all flung up their arms and they screamed too.

"EEEEEEAAAAWWWWAAAAGGHH!"

Goldilocks thought she was going to be eaten! She leaped out of bed and dived out of the nearest window. She landed in a blackberry bush, picked herself up, and ran off home as fast as her legs would go.

After The Three Bears got over their shock, Father Bear
made some more porridge, Mother Bear mended Baby
Bear's chair and Baby Bear made the beds.

They lived happily ever after and always locked their door
when they went out, just in case.

Goldilocks never went back to The Three Bears' house. She grew up into a fine young woman and had many adventures, but she never did eat porridge again.

THE STORY OF RUMPELSTILTSKIN

Once upon a time, long, long ago, when mountains were more pointed and there was a king in every castle, there lived a miller who was forever telling tall stories. The miller had a daughter called Ruby, who was very clever, and he was always boasting about the things she could do.

Once he boasted that his daughter sang so beautifully that
the birds came out at night and flew around the moon.
Another time he said his daughter could juggle four
hedgehogs with one hand and make a dozen fruit cakes
with the other.

These stories were so silly that his neighbours just laughed when they heard them, but one day the King was in town and he heard one of the miller's stories.

"My daughter is so clever that she can spin straw into gold," the miller said.

The King loved gold and, when he heard the miller's boast, he ordered Ruby to be brought to his castle and led her to a small room where there was a spinning wheel and straw piled up to the ceiling.

"Spin this straw into gold by morning or you will be fed to the Royal Crocodiles," the King said, and locked her in.

Poor Ruby was both cross and frightened. "What has my stupid father done now. I can't spin straw into gold," she said. She looked at the straw and thought about the Royal Crocodiles and began to cry.

Suddenly a funny little man appeared and skipped around the room. "Well now, what's all this? Why are you crying?" he said.

"I must spin this straw into gold and I don't know how," answered Ruby.

The little man smiled and said, "What will you give me if I spin the straw into gold for you?"

"I will give you my necklace," said Ruby.

"Very well," said the little man and held out his hand.
Ruby gave him the necklace and he put it in his pocket.
Then he sat down at the spinning wheel and started to
spin. He really was spinning straw into gold!

All through the night the little man worked at the spinning wheel and, by morning, all the straw was gone and in its place was a heap of glistening gold thread. Ruby stared at the gold in amazement.

"Oh thank you," she said to the little man, but he'd disappeared.

When the King came and unlocked the door he gasped at
the sight of all the gold. He thought Ruby was indeed
very clever, but he was a very greedy King. That night he
took Ruby to a bigger room with a spinning wheel and
straw piled up to the ceiling.

"Spin this straw into gold by morning or you will be fed to the Royal Crocodiles," the King said, and again he locked her in.

Ruby sat at the spinning wheel and tried to spin the straw but all she made was dust. "Oh, if only that little man could help me," she cried.

"Here I am," said a voice, and there he was again. "What will you give me if I spin all this straw into gold for you?" said the funny little man.

"I will give you my ring," said Ruby, and quickly put it in his hand.

He smiled and sat down at the spinning wheel. Again the little man worked busily all night and in the morning, when all the straw was gone and in its place was a bigger heap of glistening gold, he disappeared.

At sunrise the King came and unlocked the door. He was delighted to see all the gold. "You are indeed very, very clever," he said, but he was a very, very greedy king and he wanted even more.

That night he took Ruby to an even bigger room with a spinning wheel and straw piled up to the ceiling.

"Spin this straw into gold by morning or you will be fed to the Royal Crocodiles," the King said, and once again he locked her in.

Ruby looked at the mountain of straw and said, "Oh, what am I to do? Only that little man can help me now."

"Here I am," said a voice, and once again there he was. "What will you give me if I spin all this straw into gold for you?" said the funny little man.

"I have nothing more to give you," said Ruby.

"Then promise to give me your first baby when you are Queen," said the little man.

Ruby thought this could never happen, so she promised.

Once again the little man worked all night at the spinning wheel until all the straw was gone and in its place was a huge heap of glistening gold. Then, as before, he disappeared.

Once more the King came and unlocked the door. He was overjoyed to see all the gold. "You are the cleverest in all my kingdom," he said. "Marry me and we will be rich for ever."

Ruby was a bit shocked but, since there was no more talk of crocodiles, she said, "Yes."

Soon there was a grand Royal Wedding and Ruby and the King were married. They were very happy together and, when their first baby was born, they were even happier, but Queen Ruby forgot her promise to the little man.

One day he came when Queen Ruby was alone and reminded her. She cried and cried until, at last, the little man said, "If you can guess my name in three days you can keep your child." Then he disappeared.

All day and night Ruby sat thinking of all the names she knew, and she sent messengers all over the kingdom to find new ones.

Next day, when the little man came, Queen Ruby said, "Is it Thomas, Kevin, or Michael?"

"No, no, no," said the little man, and skipped away.

The next day Queen Ruby tried more unusual names. "Is it Bandylegs, Jellybottom, or Crookshanks?"

"No, no, no," said the little man skipping away. "If you can't guess my name tomorrow, I will take the baby."

On the morning of the third day Queen Ruby was feeling very unhappy when a messenger returned and said, "Yesterday I was in the great dark wood, when I came upon a funny little house. In front of the house was a fire, and a strange little man was dancing around the fire singing:

> 'Hocus pocus, dance and sing
> First a necklace, then a ring
> Riddles and magic are my game
> RUMPELSTILTSKIN is my name!'"

Queen Ruby jumped for joy. "Thank you, thank you!" she said to the messenger and gave her a bag of gold.

When the funny little man appeared, Queen Ruby pretended not to know and said, "Is your name Jack, or is it Percy, or is it ...

R U M P E L S T I L T S K I N ? "

"Aaaaahh!! Someone told you!" shouted the little man. He jumped about, all in a rage, and stamped his foot so hard it went through the floor where it stuck fast. Red in the face, he pulled and pulled at his leg, then, with a cry of anger, he disappeared in a puff of smoke.

Ruby lived happily ever after. She was a good Queen and well loved by the people and, after the birth of her second child, it was decreed that she and her children should rule the country, leaving the King to count his treasure.

The King had a long life but one day, whilst he was carrying a heavy sack of gold, he accidentally fell into the Royal Crocodile Pool and was never seen again.

THE
THREE
BILLY GOATS
GRUFF

Once upon a time, in a land beyond the high mountains
and over the sea, there were three billy goats who lived
on a rocky hillside. There was a big billy goat, a middle-
sized billy goat, and a little billy goat, and they were all
called Gruff.

The three Billy Goats Gruff had always lived on the
hillside and every day they did nothing but eat from
morning till night. The other goats who lived there
were happy to eat the rough grass that grew between the
stones, the moss that grew on the rocks, and the leaves
and twigs that grew on the trees; but the three Billy Goats
Gruff wanted more.

They dreamed of going down into the valley, trotting across the bridge which joined the rocky hillside to the lush green meadow on the other side of the river and eating until they were fat.

But the bridge was the only way across the river, which was deep and fast flowing, and under the bridge lived a Troll. He was as frightening to look at as he was fierce and would gobble up anyone who tried to cross to the other side and no one dared to try.

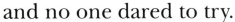

One day, when the three Billy Goats Gruff were again moaning about the coarse grass and dry leaves, an old grandfather billy goat, who was eating nearby, laughed and said,

"Perhaps you should all go and feast yourselves in the big meadow."

"Perhaps we should!" replied the little Billy Goat Gruff, cheekily.

"And what about the river?" said the grandfather billy goat. "And the Troll?"

"I'm not afraid of the Troll," said the big Billy Goat Gruff.

"Neither am I," said the middle-sized Billy Goat Gruff.

"Nor me," said the little Billy Goat Gruff. "We'll go right now!"

The other two Billy Goats Gruff looked at the little Billy
Goat Gruff, then at each other. They hadn't intended
this to happen and were rather shocked.

"Well, are all you brave Billy Goats Gruff going?"
taunted the grandfather billy goat.

"Er... yes, of course we are," said the big
Billy Goat Gruff. "We're not frightened."

Really they were all very frightened, but now they had
to go, or look foolish.

"Goodbye, Billy Goats Gruff. I don't expect we'll see
you again," said the old grandfather billy goat.

The three Billy Goats Gruff started off down the hillside, slowly at first, then faster and faster as it became a race to the bottom.

When they reached the river they looked at the deep rushing water. If only they could swim across, they all thought. They gazed over at the green meadow. It made them feel hungry, but also afraid.

They looked again across the river. The sun was shining
on the lush green grass and clover and speckles of sweet
flowers sparkled in the sunlight.

Determinedly they made their way along the river bank
to the big wooden bridge.

Standing well back, they tried to look underneath at what might be lurking in the shadows, but it was too dark and gloomy to see.

(Deep within the darkness lay the Troll asleep. He'd been fishing all night but had caught nothing, which had made him very grumpy.)

"Perhaps the Troll has gone away?" said the little Billy Goat Gruff hopefully.

"Perhaps he has," said the middle-sized Billy Goat Gruff. "Since this was your idea, you go first and see. We'll just wait here."

The middle-sized Billy Goat Gruff and the big Billy Goat Gruff stepped back, leaving the little Billy Goat Gruff standing alone.

The little Billy Goat Gruff was afraid. He turned to look at his brothers, then, with his head held high, bravely set off across the bridge.

TRIP, TRAP! TRIP, TRAP! TRIP, TRAP! TRIP, TRAP! went his hooves on the wooden boards. He was nearly in the middle and thought he was going to get safely across when suddenly the monstrous Troll popped his head out from beneath the bridge.

"Who's that trip-trapping over my bridge?" roared the Troll, rubbing his eyes.

"It's only me," said the little Billy Goat Gruff in his little voice, "I'm going across to the meadow to make myself fat."

"Oh no you're not!" roared the Troll. "You've woken me up and now I'm coming to gobble you up!"

"No, no, don't eat me," bleated the little Billy Goat Gruff. "I'm the littlest Billy Goat Gruff. I'm too small and bony. Wait until the second Billy Goat Gruff comes along. He's much bigger and fatter."

"Very well," said the Troll angrily, "be off with you!"

So the little Billy Goat Gruff crossed the bridge and skipped off into the meadow to eat the sweet grass.

When the middle-sized Billy Goat Gruff saw that his brother had reached the meadow safely, he felt much braver and he too set off across the bridge.

TRIP, TRAP! TRIP, TRAP! TRIP, TRAP! TRIP, TRAP! went his hooves on the wooden boards. He was nearly in the middle when again out popped the Troll's head, looking very fierce, from beneath the bridge.

"Who's that trip-trapping over my bridge?" roared the Troll.

"It's only me," said the middle-sized Billy Goat Gruff in his middle-sized voice. "I'm going across to the meadow to make myself fat."

"Oh no you're not!" roared the Troll. "I'm coming to gobble you up!"

"No, no, don't eat me," pleaded the middle-sized Billy Goat Gruff. "I'm not a very big Billy Goat Gruff. There's a much bigger one than me. Wait until the third Billy Goat Gruff comes along. He's much bigger and fatter."

"Very well," said the Troll even angrier, "be off with you!"

So the middle-sized Billy Goat Gruff crossed the bridge and skipped off into the meadow to join his brother eating the sweet grass.

Then there was only the big Billy Goat Gruff left to cross. He puffed himself up to make him feel very strong and brave, then he too set off across the bridge.

TRIP, TRAP! TRIP, TRAP! TRIP, TRAP! TRIP, TRAP! stamped his hooves on the wooden boards. He was nearly in the middle when, once again, out popped the Troll's head looking fiercer than ever.

"Who's that trip-trapping over my bridge?" roared the Troll.

"It's me, the biggest Billy Goat Gruff," bellowed the big Billy Goat Gruff in his great big voice, "and I'm going across to the meadow to make myself fat!"

"Oh no you're not!" roared the Troll, even
louder than before, "I'm coming to gobble
you up!"

The Troll leapt up onto the bridge and started gnashing his teeth but the big Billy Goat Gruff stamped his hooves, then lowered his horns, and charged!

Thundering over the wooden boards, with steam coming out of his nostrils, he tossed the Troll high in the air. Up, up he went, so high he circled the moon, then down, down he fell – SPLASH! – into the middle of the deep river and was never seen again.

The Big Billy Goat Gruff crossed the bridge and skipped off into the meadow to join his brothers.

Then the three Billy Goats Gruff ate the sweet grass until they were fat, and then they ate until their tummies hurt, and then they ate until they couldn't move, and then they went to sleep for a long, long time.

The three Billy Goats Gruff had a long and happy life. They all grew up to be old grandfather Billy Goats Gruff with great curling horns and long grey beards.

Sometimes they went back over the bridge to see their friends on the rocky hillside, but whenever they did, they galloped across as fast as they could just in case the Troll had come back.

THE
PRINCESS
AND THE
FROG

Once upon a time, long ago, when the world was not as it always has been and rivers flowed uphill as well as down, there lived a king who had seven daughters. The six elder daughters had each gone to seek their way in the world, only Ivy, the youngest daughter, still lived at home.

Ivy was not like her older sisters, who were very fine and sensible and enjoyed doing royal things such as wearing crowns and going to grand balls. Ivy was happiest playing in the fields and woods that surrounded her father's castle. She especially liked to play with the beautiful, shiny, golden ball which her father had given her. It was the most treasured of all her possessions.

One bright sunny morning Ivy gulped down her breakfast, then ran out of the castle and into the fields, kicking her golden ball ahead of her. She ran across one field, then another, until she reached the edge of the big wood where she kicked the ball as hard as she could. Ivy watched as it rose high in the air, over the top of some smaller trees, then down through the branches of a tall oak until it fell - SPLASH! - into the middle of a deep pool where it sank out of sight.

Quickly Ivy found a long stick and prodded around in the pool, but she couldn't feel the ball anywhere and all she fished out was mud and weed.

Ivy was feeling desperate and began to cry.

"BOO HOO HOO!" she wailed and sobbed.

Then she heard a voice saying, "Princess, why are you crying?" Ivy looked around to see where the voice was coming from. All she could see was a green frog sitting on a rock by the pool.

"Did you say something?" said Ivy.

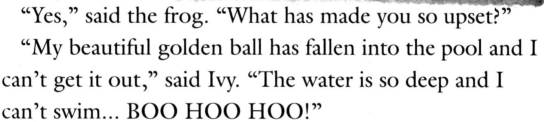

"Yes," said the frog. "What has made you so upset?"

"My beautiful golden ball has fallen into the pool and I can't get it out," said Ivy. "The water is so deep and I can't swim... BOO HOO HOO!"

"Don't cry," said the frog. "I can find your ball. But what will you give me if I do?"

"I will give you anything you want," said Ivy. "You can have my jewels, my fancy royal clothes, even my best crown, if only you will find my golden ball."

"I do not want your jewels or your clothes or even your golden crown. I want to be your friend. I want to sit beside you at the table, eat from your golden plate and drink from your golden cup. I want to sleep on a silk cushion beside your pretty bed. And I want you to kiss me goodnight before you sleep. If you promise me these things," said the frog, "I will find your golden ball."

Ivy thought the frog was talking a lot of nonsense but she wanted her golden ball so much she was willing to agree to anything.

"I promise all you ask," she said, "if only you will find my golden ball."

The frog smiled and said, "Remember, you've promised." Then he dived down deep into the pool.

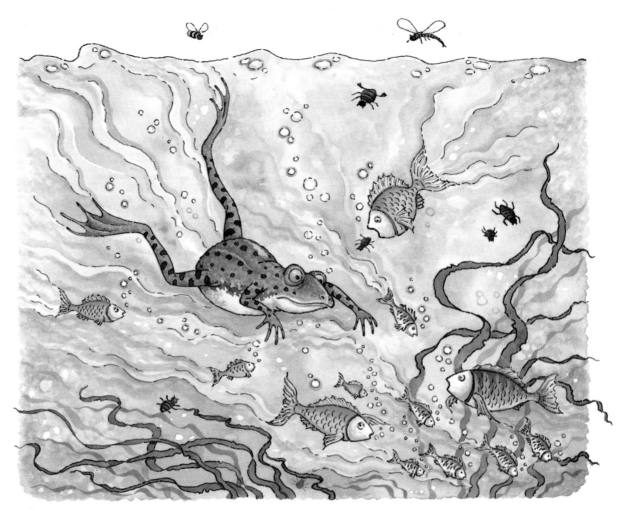

After a long time the frog came swimming up again with the golden ball. Ivy was overjoyed!

The frog threw the ball on to the grass beside Ivy and she picked it up and hugged it. Then she turned and ran off home as fast as she could.

Quickly the frog hopped out of the water.

"Wait for me! Wait for me!" he croaked.

He hopped along trying to catch up but was soon left far behind. Without looking back Ivy kept on running across the fields towards her father's castle.

A week and a day later Ivy had forgotten all about the frog. She was sitting at dinner with the King and all his courtiers when a messenger entered the great hall and announced, "Your Majesty, there is a frog at the door who says that Princess Ivy promised to share her dinner with him."

Ivy looked shocked and her face turned red.

"Is this true, Ivy?" said the King, looking very surprised.

"Well... it is a bit true," said Ivy. Then she told her father what had happened in the big wood and what the frog had asked of her. "I promised him that he could come and live with me," she said, "but I never thought he would follow me all the way home. I don't want to live with a slimy old frog."

The King was a good and honest man who never told a lie and always kept his word. He shook his head and said, "My dear, when a promise is made it must be kept. You must ask the frog to dine with you."

Ivy felt ashamed and reluctantly asked the messenger to show the frog in.

Presently the frog hopped into the great hall and sat by Ivy's chair.

"You promised I could sit beside you," said the frog. Ivy couldn't bear to touch the frog so she picked it up with her napkin and put it on the table. The frog smiled at her and sat beside her plate.

Ivy called for a servant to bring some beetles and pondweed for him but the frog said, "No, I want to eat what you eat, Princess. You promised I could eat from your golden plate and drink from your golden cup."

The thought of this made Ivy feel quite sick and she didn't want to eat any more. The frog, however, enjoyed every bite.

When he had finished the frog said to Ivy, "Now I'm tired, please take me to your room."

Ivy turned to the King and said, "Do I have to?" The King looked at her sternly and said, "Yes, you do. The frog helped you when you were in need and you made him a promise."

So Ivy carried the frog to her bedroom, but as she passed her maid she whispered, "Bring a fishtank with a lid to my bedroom, now."

When the maid brought the fishtank (in which she'd put a stone and some tadpoles to keep the frog company) Ivy quickly popped the frog inside and shut the lid, then she climbed into bed.

"No, no, no," said the frog, jumping up and down, "you promised I could sleep on a silk cushion beside your bed!" And he jumped up and down so much he knocked the lid off the fishtank and hopped out. "If you don't put me on a cushion beside your bed I shall tell the King you do not keep your promises."

Ivy remembered what her father had said. With tears in her eyes she picked up the frog and put him on a silk cushion beside her bed. How unhappy she was. She didn't want to live with a green frog for the rest of her life!

"Now kiss me goodnight," the frog said.

"Oh, how horrible!" thought Ivy, but again, she knew her father would insist. Trying to pretend she was somewhere else, she leaned over, closed her eyes, pursed her lips... and kissed the frog...

Suddenly the room was filled with bright lights and stars! Ivy opened her eyes and couldn't believe what she saw. The frog had disappeared! He had turned into a handsome prince!

"Oh thank you, thank you!" he said. Then he told Ivy how a wicked witch had put a spell on him and turned him into a frog. The spell could only be broken if a beautiful princess would befriend him, eat with him, sleep beside him and kiss him.

The Frog Prince, whose name was Frederick, told Princess Ivy how he had seen her playing with her golden ball in the wood and had fallen in love with her.

Princess Ivy blushed. "We must tell my father what has happened," she said. The King was very surprised when he saw Prince Frederick with Ivy but he was so glad that she was not going to live with a frog.

Princess Ivy and Prince Freddy, as he was better known, became the best of friends and were always together. On sunny days they played in the fields with Princess Ivy's golden ball, or in the wood where Prince Freddy taught Princess Ivy how to swim; and on wet days they played indoors with Prince Freddy's aquarium.

After a year and a day Princess Ivy and Prince Freddy were married. The King was delighted and there were celebrations throughout the land. Within seven years the Princess and Prince had seven children, who were surprisingly good at both swimming and leapfrog, and they all lived happily ever after.

THE
UGLY DUCKLING

Once upon a time, on a dark and stormy night, a great wild wind blew down from the hills. It whistled through the woods and across the fields to the river where it blew a poor mother duck right out of her nest.

"Oh dear," she said, picking herself up, "I must get back to my eggs!"

She stumbled around in the dark until she found her nest then, exhausted, she settled down again on the eggs to keep them warm.

In the morning the storm had passed and the sun came up warm and bright. The mother-duck awoke when she felt something move beneath her.

The eggs were rocking to and fro. She counted them, "One, two, three, four, five, six ... seven?" She had only laid six eggs but now there were seven, and one was much bigger than the rest.

"I don't remember that one," she said. "Seven eggs, I am a lucky duck!"

Soon, one by one, the smaller eggs broke open and out popped six pretty little yellow ducklings. But the biggest egg had not hatched.

The six ducklings gathered around the big egg and
watched as the mother duck sat on top of it for a day and
a night until the egg, at last, began to stir. Slowly it cracked
open and out tumbled a big scruffy duckling with grey
feathers and very big black feet.

   "Oh my," said the mother duck, "you are a funny one!"
   The other six ducklings were a little afraid of their new
brother and scurried under the mother duck to hide.
They peered out at the big grey duckling as he wobbled
out of his shell, gazed around at the world and smiled.

   "Oh well," said the mother duck, "he looks happy and
healthy," and cuddled him to her with the other ducklings.

Next day the mother duck led her new family down to the river for a swimming lesson. The six little yellow ducklings scampered down the bank after their mother while the big grey duckling followed clumsily behind. One by one they jumped in the water. The yellow ducklings struggled and splashed but the grey duckling found his big feet very useful and he swam straight away. The other ducklings tried to keep up with him but the big duckling was much too fast.

"Oh well," said the mother duck, "he may not be a beauty but he can certainly swim."

One day the mother duck took her ducklings to visit some friends in the farmyard. The farm ducks were thrilled to see the new yellow ducklings.

"What little beauties!" they said, fussing around and patting them. Then they saw the big grey duckling.

"What is that?" said one old duck.

"What a strange awkward creature," said another.

The big grey duckling became shy and hid behind his mother but she was proud of all her offspring and urged him on saying, "And this is my big strong son."

The big duckling stuck out his chest and stepped forward but tripped over his feet and fell head first in a muddy puddle. The farm ducks all laughed, "Ha, ha, ha, what a mess!"

The mother duck tried to help him. "Leave him alone!" she said. "He may not be pretty but he's gentle and brave." But the other ducks rolled about laughing.

"Ha, ha, ha, what a clumsy cluck! What an ugly duckling!"

Other animals came over to see what the joke was. When the hens saw the big duckling they laughed too, and so did the pigs, and the sheep, and the cow, and the horse.

The duckling looked around at all the laughing animals and frowned.

"I don't belong here!" he said and ran out of the farmyard and away across the fields.

The duckling ran on and on until he came to the great marsh where the wild ducks live. He was tired and sat down to rest in a clump of reeds.

"I know I'm not little, yellow and fluffy like my brothers and sisters," he said to himself. "But I'm me! I may be scruffy and grey and I may have big black feet, but I'm as good as they are."

Three wild ducks were flying past and saw him sitting in the reeds.

"Look, there's a mumbling duckling with big feet!" said one and they all laughed.

The duckling looked up and stuck his tongue out at them, he didn't care. The wild ducks flew away laughing loudly. "See you again flipper feet," they called.

"I'll show them," said the duckling.

He fell asleep and dreamed he was with other ducklings just like himself, but suddenly – BANG! BANG! BANG! – the duckling awoke with a start. Men were shooting at ducks all around!

He put his wings over his head and tried to hide but then something came rushing towards him through the marsh – a huge dog with a big red tongue and sharp teeth!

The duckling jumped into a pool and hid under the water until the dog had gone.

"I don't belong here!" said the duckling. "This is a terrible place!" and he hurried away from the marsh.

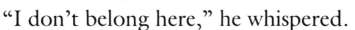As darkness fell he came to the big wood. Strange noises
and shadows seemed to follow him as he waddled along
the path through the tall trees.

"I don't belong here," he whispered.

Soon he came to a tumbledown cottage where a light
shone from a window. The house belonged to an old
woman who lived with her cat and a hen. The duckling
was cold and tired and he could see it was warm inside,
so he crept in through a crack in the door.

The old woman was pleased to see him. "Now I shall
have eggs from a duck as well as a hen," she said, and
made a place for the duckling by the fire.

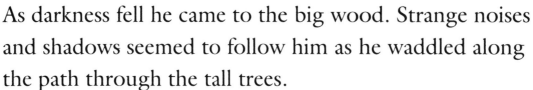

When the old woman went to bed the cat and the hen cornered the duckling.

"Can you lay eggs?" said the hen.

"No," said the duckling, "but I can swim."

"Can you purr?" said the cat.

"No," replied the duckling, "but I can dive."

"Swim and dive indeed! You're no use to our mistress," they both said.

"I don't care!" said the duckling and waddled out of the door and into the night. "I don't belong here," he said.

The duckling journeyed on and on over hills and dales looking for a place to call home. Eventually he found a small lake where he lived on his own and no one bothered him.

Many weeks passed and the leaves on the trees turned from green to brown. The days were shorter and the duckling shivered through the long nights.

One evening, as the sun was setting, he heard a strange sound in the sky and looked up to see a flock of the most beautiful birds. They were magical white birds with great outstretched wings and long graceful necks.

One of them gave a strange cry that he seemed to understand and he wished he could go with them.

Soon the cold winds of winter blew and the lake, where the duckling lived, began to freeze. He swam round and round to keep warm but the water froze around his feet and he was stuck fast.

Next morning a kind farmer passed by and saw the duckling. He smashed the ice and carried the frozen bird home and put him by the fire to warm up. The duckling felt happy and safe but when the farmer's children came home they were noisy and frightened him.

He flapped his wings to try to get away from them and knocked over a bowl of milk. Their mother tried to catch him but he flew into the butter tub and then fell in the flour barrel. Milk, butter and flour were spilled all over the floor! The farmer shouted, the mother shouted, the children shouted too!

"I don't belong here!" said the duckling, and ran out of the door.

On and on he ran through the snow until he could run no more and there he curled up in a hollow and slept for the rest of the long cold winter.

He awoke beside a large lake with the sun on his back and the larks singing overhead. Spring had come at last. The grass was green, there was blossom on the trees, and he was feeling much stronger.

He wandered down to the water and swam away from the bank. He was enjoying himself when, from behind some tall rushes, sailed three of the beautiful white birds he had seen flying so high, and they were coming towards him. He thought they were going to call him names as most animals did so he puffed himself up ready for them, but instead they greeted him warmly.

"Hello brother, you are new to these parts."

The ugly duckling thought they were talking to someone else and bowed his head in confusion. Then he saw his reflection in the still water.

He was no longer scruffy, grey and clumsy. He was big and white and graceful and ... just like the beautiful birds who were talking to him!

"What am I?" he said to the three swans.

246

"Why you're a swan, and a very handsome one too," they replied.

"A swan, a swan! I'm not an ugly duckling, I'm a swan!" he cried.

The duckling swan lived happily ever after. The three older swans became his best friends and they swam and flew everywhere together.

One day he was flying over the riverbank when he saw his mother with a new family of ducklings (every one a duck this time). He flew down and told her his story. She was delighted with his good fortune and very proud of him. From then on, whenever she saw a swan flying high above her in the sky, she would say to her ducklings, or anyone else who would listen, "That's probably my son up there."

First published in hardback in Great Britain by HarperCollins Publishers Ltd in 1997
This edition published by HarperCollins Children's Books in 2006

1 3 5 7 9 10 8 6 4 2
ISBN-13: 978-0-00-198292-5
ISBN-10: 0-00-198292-3

First published by HarperCollins Publishers Ltd as *Collins Bedtime Treasury of Nursery Rhymes and Tales* in 1997
and as *The Collins Book of Nursery Rhymes* in 1990 and *The Collins Book of Nursery Tales* in 1993

The Collins Book of Nursery Rhymes
Collections copyright © William Collins Sons & Co Ltd 1981
Illustrations copyright © William Collins Sons & Co Ltd 1980

The Collins Book of Nursery Tales
Compilation copyright © HarperCollins Publishers Ltd 1993
Text and illustrations copyright © Jonathan Langley 1991, 1992, 1993

Printed and bound in Thailand